FOUND BY THE MOUNTAIN MAN

WILD HEART MOUNTAIN: MILITARY HEROES
BOOK FOUR

SADIE KING

FOUND BY THE MOUNTAIN MAN

A woman on the run and an ex-sniper who'll do anything to protect her...

I've been an orphan, a delinquent, a Marine, and a sniper. But I've never been in love until I stumble upon the lost girl sheltering in the forest.

She's battered and bruised on the outside with more scars on the inside.

I take her in. I heal her. And when she tells me about her past, I do what I do best: whatever it takes to protect her.

I was a Scout Sniper in the Marines. I'm not looking for redemption. I'm looking for revenge.

Found by the Mountain Man is a found-family, age gap, instalove romance featuring an ex-military mountain man and the curvy, innocent woman he claims as his own.

RHYS

The deer raises her head to nibble a berry bush, giving me the perfect shot at her elegant neck. Slowly, I raise my hunting rifle to my shoulder and ease off the safety.

I line up the crosshairs to the point at the base of her neck where her spine begins. It's an awkward shot. A precise hit results in quick death, a slight deviation causes slow agony. But I never miss, or at least I never used to.

Except today my fingers tremble as I rest them on the trigger. The vibrations cause the rifle to shake.

Memories of different gun sites and different targets flood my brain. I never missed a shot when I was in the Marines. I've seen men crumple seconds after I pull the trigger, the life bleeding out of them.

My hand shakes, and I curse under my breath.

It's a deer, not a human.

But I can't get my hands to stop trembling.

I take a big breath and let it out again, trying to steady myself.

The crosshairs are jumping, making it hard to line up the shot. But if I wait any longer, the deer will move on and I'll miss my moment.

I used to be able to shoot with my eyes closed and still hit a bullseye. It was that party trick that got me noticed in the Marines. It got me into the elite Scout Sniper training, a rigorous course that got me qualified as a HOG, Hunter of Gunmen, and got me a position as the Scout Sniper for my unit.

I close my eyes and pull the trigger.

The blast shatters the silence of the forest, birds scatter, and the deer bucks and takes off into the undergrowth.

The bullet didn't even graze her.

Frustration boils inside me. Three years after leaving the military, and not being able to do the one thing I was good at still hurts.

Thick raindrops spatter the foliage around me, and I peer up at the sky. The thick cloud that's been hanging over the mountain all morning is finally breaking. Slinging my rifle over my shoulder, I zip up my parka and trudge back though the forest.

I'm a mile or so southeast of my cabin. I only

came out to check my traps, but when I saw the deer scat, I tracked it to this spot.

The rain gets heavier as I hike back. The canopy of trees provides some cover, but it's heavy enough to get me soaked within a few minutes.

I'm walking with my head down, so I almost miss the woman. It's her red cloak that draws my attention. Bright colors are rare in the forest.

She's huddled under a giant sycamore tree. Her knees are tucked up to her chest, and her hands are clasped around her knees. Her dark hair is soaking wet and plastered to her skull.

I look around, but no one else is in the forest. Even the animals are sheltering from the downpour.

"Hey."

She doesn't hear me, so I go closer and plant my feet right in front of hers. That gets her attention. Her head tilts from my boot-clad feet, up my legs and torso until her eyes meet mine.

Her face leaves me breathless. She's startlingly beautiful and terrifyingly messed up.

The skin around her left eye is swollen and bruised, and there are scratches on her pale face. Rain runs in rivulets down her cheeks and drips off her swollen lips.

"Are you okay?"

She opens her mouth, but no sound comes out.

She unclasps a hand from her knees and holds it

out to me. It's a feeble gesture, and I'm not sure if she's reaching for me or trying to fend me off.

Whichever it is, the action proves too much for her. The woman's eyes roll back in her head, and she slides sideways.

I catch her just before she hits the forest floor.

Her body is limp and cold, and her clothing drenched. Whoever she is, wherever she came from, she needs my help. I can't abandon her in the forest during a rainstorm.

I slide my arms around her and lift her up. One arm goes around her shoulders and the other goes under her legs.

Her body's soft with feminine curves, and as I pull her toward my chest, something stirs inside of me.

Mine.

I don't know who this woman is or where she came from, but I found her, and she's mine.

She's still unconscious as I carry her back to my cabin.

2

INDIGO

It doesn't smell right. There's no stench of pig shit, no snuffles from the porcine friends I share the sleeping pen with. And the straw is softer. It doesn't feel like straw at all. It feels like…

My eyes fly open wondering whose bed I'm in. A man I don't recognize sits with a rifle on his lap.

His eyes are closed, and his chest rises and falls rhythmically. He's asleep with both hands on the rifle.

The last few days flash before me. The woods, the hunger, my body growing weaker, and then this man. I think I fainted and came to bumping up against his solid chest as he carried me through the rain.

I study the man as he dozes.

He's in a sweater that's pushed up to the elbow,

showing off thick, muscular forearms decorated in multicolored tattoos. The tattoos cover his forearms and disappear under the sweater to reappear on his neck. It's a good look and goes with his scruffy beard and shoulder length curly dark hair.

He's the kind of guy I might chat up in a bar, back in my old life when I went to bars.

He's beautiful in a real kind of way, with lines around his eyes and flashes of silver in his hair.

Who is he?

All I remember is the rain coming down and sheltering under a tree thinking this was it. Wondering if I was better off going back to where I'd come from. The thought makes me shudder, and I stick to my conclusion: I'd rather die in the woods than go back there..

But here I am, under guard in a strange mountain man's cabin. Who knows what his plans are for me. Maybe I've jumped from the frying pan into the fire.

Quietly, so as not to make the bed squeak, I sit up and survey my surroundings. I'm in a bedroom of a log cabin. There's a single window with the curtains half drawn. The rain has stopped, and judging by the light it's sometime around midday. Behind the man is a door, which is shut, so the window might be my best chance of escape.

My clothes are hanging over a second chair by

the window. The rain and mud are washed off, but there's no hiding the tears in the fabric.

How long have I been here?

And if my clothes are over there, what am I wearing?

I glance down at my chest, and I'm in a black t-shirt with a Metallica emblem on the front. It's not mine. I pull back the blankets, and the t-shirt is so big on me that it falls to my knees. I peel it off my thighs and oh my god. I'm not wearing any panties.

I gasp. They must be with my freshly laundered clothes.

Did the man undress me?

Heat prickles my skin and creeps up my neck, flushing it pink. A stranger has seen me naked. But what's more disconcerting is the reaction in my body. The thought that this man saw my body is not entirely unpleasant.

The realization that he undressed me while I was semi-conscious should make my skin crawl, but instead my core tightens and my nipples harden.

I need to get a grip.

I'm in a strange bed, in a strange cabin, with a strange man with a gun guarding me.

I don't know how the hell I manage to get myself into these situations, but it's time to get the hell out of here.

I slide over to the side of the bed and pause when

I see what's on the bedside table. A sandwich. White bread with thick pieces of ham and cheese with mayonnaise oozing out the side.

My stomach growls, and my mouth salivates. I haven't eaten since my supplies ran out in the woods. And those supplies consisted of one apple and some berries that I saw a deer eating and figured must be safe.

There's a glass of chocolate milk next to the sandwich, which almost makes me whimper. Chocolate milk and a ham and cheese sandwich. There is no way I'm leaving before consuming those.

I take a huge bite of sandwich, and as soon as the food hits my taste buds, all decorum goes out the window. I stuff the food into my mouth, not able to chew fast enough. With the sandwich still in my mouth, I gulp down the chocolate milk. In my hurry, some of it dribbles out the corner of my mouth. I wipe it with the back of my hand as I glance up at the man.

His eyes are open, and he's staring straight at me.

3

RHYS

he woman gulps down the sandwich like
it's the first food she's had in days.

When she sees me watching, panic flares in her
eyes and she scrambles out of bed. But her legs are
weak, and she stumbles before finding the wall to
prop her up.

"Who the fuck are you?"

Wow. My girl has a mouth on her like a soldier.

"I'm Rhys Winters."

Her eyes dart to the gun. It can't be a good look,
but I always keep my gun by my side. It's a habit
from the military.

I lift my hands off the rifle in a placating gesture.

"I'm not gonna hurt you. I want to help you."

She eyes me suspiciously while keeping her back
up against the wall. She looks like a caged animal,

and a flare of anger goes through me as I wonder what's got her so scared.

"What's your name?"

Her eyes narrow. "Who got me dressed?"

Her clothes were sodden when I got her back to my place, and she was in and out of consciousness. I couldn't put her to bed in wet things, and she wasn't with it enough to dress herself.

"I did."

Her eyebrows knit together even further if that's possible.

"Your clothes were wet; I didn't want you to catch a fever. I put the t-shirt on before I took off your…" I look away. I may have had a shitty childhood, but I was brought up to respect a lady.

"…underthings."

The memory of her pale white skin flashes into my mind. I held her up with one arm while I pulled her soaking dress off, trying not to peek at her bra and panties as I slid my t-shirt over her head. Then fumbling underneath the t-shirt to pull her wet things off. I had a hard-on by the time I finished, but I'm not going to tell her that.

She harrumphs, which I take as a sign she's accepted the explanation.

"I found you in the woods during a heavy rainfall. You looked lost. But if you've got somewhere you need to be, you can leave anytime."

She doesn't detect the hitch in my voice. If she walks out the door right now, I'll follow her and find out how to make her mine. I don't want her to go, but I need to give her the option.

She looks away and wraps her arms around her middle. The t-shirt rides up her thighs, and I fight every urge not to stare.

The woman doesn't say anything, and I take the silence to mean she doesn't have a place to go. Which is what I suspected.

When we got back here, I called my buddy Symon to ask if there were any women reported missing. He's a ranger on Wild Heart Mountain and will know about any hikers or campers that haven't made it back. But no one on the mountain has reported a missing woman.

She wasn't dressed for hiking with her red cloak and old-fashioned tunic. And from the way she devoured that sandwich, I bet she hasn't eaten in a while.

But it's the black eye that has me agitated. Someone did that to her, and when I find out who it was, they'll be sorry. But if she's not ready to tell me her name, then it's not yet the time to ask about her injuries.

"I've got some rabbit stew that needs heating up, if you're still hungry."

She turns her gaze back to me. Her dark eyes are less haunted, less suspicious.

"Is that what you eat in the mountains? Rabbit?"

She's not from around here. I store the piece of information away and give her what I hope is a reassuring smile.

"I caught and skinned it myself."

She frowns at me again. "Gross."

I chuckle. What's a girl like her doing on her own up the mountain?

"It's a good feeling, eating something you killed yourself. It's honest."

She tilts her head at me thoughtfully.

"I guess."

"I'm a trapper up here on the mountain. I trap animals and sell the meat and pelts in town." I'm not used to talking so much, but I figure if I keep rambling on it will put her at ease. "Mostly rabbits and some squirrels. Occasionally foxes during the season."

"Do you hunt?"

The question gives me pause. I think of the deer this morning and my trembling hands. And I think of the men I hunted in Iraq.

"Not anymore."

I don't want to think about Iraq, or my hands might start shaking. I stand up abruptly.

"I'm going to run you a bath. Have a soak while I get the stew heating up."

I head into the bathroom and get the tub filling, leaving my gun on the chair. If she wants to bolt, at least she'll have a weapon. But when I come back into the room a few moments later, she's sitting on the bed staring out the window. The faint colors of a rainbow arc in the pale grey sky over the forest.

"How long have I been out?"

"It's been a day and a half since I brought you in."

Her head jerks around to me. "That long?"

I nod. Apart from laundering her clothes and making inquiries, I've not left her side. My ass is sore from sitting in the chair so long, but I'm not complaining. I got to watch her sleep, and that makes it worthwhile.

"Anyone come looking for me?"

There's an edge to her voice, giving away her anxiousness. She's running from someone, but as long as she's here, I'll keep her safe.

"No. And I wouldn't let them take you if they did."

She looks at me for a long time. She must see something that makes her trust me, because her features relax.

"My name's Indigo."

"Indigo," I repeat. "Like a rainbow."

A ghost of a smile flickers across her face. I don't

know if it's her real name, but it's pretty and it suits her.

"Something like that."

"There're towels in the bathroom, Indigo. Help yourself to anything you need."

I take the gun and shut the door behind me. A wave of protectiveness hits me that's so strong I lean against the back of the door.

Indigo's mine to care for and mine to protect. I still don't know anything about her, but I know she's mine.

4

INDIGO

Hot water gushes over my body, making my skin tingle. Back at the compound, it was cold showers only in a communal unisex shower block. No matter how hard I scrubbed, I couldn't get the smell of the pigsty off of me.

Compared to the sterile concrete block at the compound, Rhys's shower is divine.

I lather up his bar of soap and scrub all over. My skin smarts in places from a hundred bruises, and there are little cuts on my hands and face from where I crawled through the fence to escape.

Once I'm out of the shower and dried off, I examine myself in the mirror. My eye is swollen and bruised so much I hardly recognize myself.

I look hideous. Beaten and bruised and worn out.

Rhys must have a hundred questions, but I'm not ready to tell him yet. I feel safe here, and he seems genuine, but I've learned people can seem one thing and be another.

If I can lay low here for a few days, it will give me an opportunity to get my strength back and figure out my next move. Whatever that is.

I left without any of my belongings. No phone, no ID, nothing. My one backpack of belongings was tucked into my cubicle in the women's living quarters. I wonder if it's still there or if they've thrown it in the trash. One more girl who passed through, got churned up, and spat out.

As I step out of the bathroom, a delicious aroma wafts from the kitchen. My stomach rumbles even though it wasn't long ago that I scarfed that sandwich.

Rhys has left out a fresh t-shirt on the bed and a pair of sweatpants. I'm a curvy girl, but the pants are enormous on me even with the cord pulled tight.

This one's a Slipknot t-shirt with tour dates on the back. I press my nose to the fabric and breathe deeply. It's a manly aroma of the forest and rain and gun oil.

A new tingle spreads over my body. My core tightens, and there's heat between my legs. I don't even know this man, but his t-shirt is turning me on. I need to get a grip.

I get changed quickly and go find him in the kitchen.

Rhys is humming to himself as he stirs a large pot on the stove. His back is to me, and it makes me stop dead in my tracks.

While I was in the shower, Rhys got the fire going, and the blaze has heated up the cabin so much that he's pulled off his sweater. Underneath is a tight fitting black t-shirt.

It hugs the muscles on his back, riding up as he leans over the stove to reveal a tantalizing line of tanned skin, taut with muscle. The biceps in his arm bulge with every stir of the wooden spoon, making his tattoos shimmer. I never thought cooking a stew could be so sexy, but *wow*.

I grip the bench to keep my legs from giving out. Heat races to my pussy, and if I was wearing panties, they'd be damp. But I'm in Rhys's sweats, which only makes me more turned on.

I let out a half whimper and half squeak which makes him turn around. He smiles when he sees me. And wow, his smile is *devastating*.

If I wasn't drenched before, I am now. I clench my thighs together, hoping he doesn't notice what effect he's having on me.

"Feel better?"

"Yup."

My voice comes out strained, and I clear my

throat. Without asking, he fetches me a glass of orange juice.

"Sit."

He places it on the kitchen counter next to a bar stool and I take a seat, trying to get my composure back. I don't even know the guy, and he's got my hormones racing all over the place.

"Can I help with anything?"

It's bad enough he's rescued me in the woods and taken me in. Now he's making me dinner.

"You need to rest. It'll take a few days to get your strength back. You can stay here as long as you need."

His kindness brings a sting to my eyes. I stand up so he doesn't see and take a look around the cabin.

It's a classic wooden cabin with an open plan kitchen and living area. Two steps lead up to the bedroom and bathroom. It's a cabin made for one. And judging by the sparse furnishing and décor, it's made for a single man.

"Do you live here alone?"

My chest constricts as I wait for his answer. The thought of a woman living here with Rhys makes me uneasy, and I'm glad when he nods his head.

"Just me."

There's a floor to ceiling fireplace on one wall with a glass fronted gun cabinet next to it. I wander over to take a look. It's quite the collection.

Five different types of rifles are mounted in the case.

Rhys is into heavy metal and guns. Exactly the type of man you want taking you back to his cabin. Yet I'm more at ease with Rhys than I have been with any other person I've come across since they took me away from my mom.

Underneath the guns is a photograph of men in military uniforms. A Marine unit by the look of the colors.

"You're in the military?"

"I was," he calls from the kitchen.

That makes sense. It explains the guns and hunting and living out here alone. I squint at the photo until I pick out Rhys amongst the men.

"Was this your unit?"

I don't realize he's come up behind me until he speaks.

"Yeah. Some of the guys live here, on the mountain." I straighten up, and he's so close behind me his breath tickles my neck. "Knowing they're close is the only thing that keeps me sane sometimes."

He says it lightly, but it makes me want to know about his military life. I'm about to ask him more when he abruptly changes the subject.

"Dinner's ready."

There's a small table near the kitchen, and he sets two steaming bowls down. I try to eat slowly this time, but the stew is so good and I can't help slurping it down.

Rhys tells me how he built the cabin with the help of his former Marine buddies. He chats easily, and I'm grateful for it. It's reassuring to know he has friends on the mountain and isn't some weird recluse. And it keeps the conversation away from me.

He tells me about how they meet up in town every month and about Angie's bar, run by the widow of one of their fallen comrades.

I like listening to him talk. I like the sound of his friends and the way they check in on each other and help each other out.

There's a pang of something in my chest. It's not quite jealousy, but a yearning to belong somewhere the way that he does. I wish I had a group of people looking out for me, or even just one person.

As we come to the end of the stew, Rhys sets his spoon down and turns his chocolate-colored eyes on me.

"Who did that to you, Indigo?"

It's the first time he's mentioned the black eye, and the abrupt change of subject takes me by surprise. I twirl my spoon around in my bowl, keeping my eyes downcast.

I want to tell him all about the compound, but I can't be sure I trust him yet. He's been kind and he seems genuine and it seems safe here, but it could all be a lie. I've trusted people before, and look where it got me.

"If you're running from someone, I need to know so I can keep you safe."

I don't say anything, and Rhys sits back on his chair.

"You don't have to tell me who it is, but if you're running from something nod your head."

My whole life I've been running from something. Ever since I turned sixteen and left the last foster care place. I thought a handsy foster kid was bad, but it was nothing compared to what happened at the compound.

But even before I got into the system, I was on the run with Mom. We were always running from one dealer boyfriend or another. She'd promise to stay clean only to hook up with another dealer somewhere else.

"Yeah." I nod. "I'm running from something."

I've been running my whole life. And I'm exhausted. I want to curl up in a safe place, a place where I can stay forever. I'm not sure that even exists.

Rhys nods briskly. "You're safe here, Indigo."

I start at the unfamiliar name. But it's growing on me.

"I mean it. You stay here as long as you need. I'll

help you heal and rest, and when you're ready, maybe you'll tell me your story."

His kindness is touching. I do feel safe here. Rhys has a way of putting me at ease. He doesn't pry, and I'm thankful for that.

"Thank you."

He stands up, and I'm relived he's not pushing me to talk when I'm not ready.

I bring the dishes over to the sink where he's running hot water. As he takes the plates from me, his hands are trembling. He dunks them in the water, and I wonder if I imagined it. But a few moments later, his hands shake so badly he knocks one of the other plates as he's putting a dish on the rack. I pretend not to notice and go wipe the table down, giving him the time he needs to compose himself.

But it makes me wonder what he did in the military and what the military did to him.

5

RHYS

It's been four days and three nights since I carried Indigo into my cabin. Since she came to, I've given her privacy at night, and instead of sleeping in the chair, I've taken up a post outside the bedroom, sleeping on the floor with my shotgun across my lap.

I don't know what she's running from, but if they turn up here, I'm not taking any chances. I'll defend her to the death if I have to.

Every time I look at her bruised eye, a surge of anger pulses through me. I've kept it hidden from her because she's as skittish as a newborn deer, looking over her shoulder and peeking out the window as if she expects to see someone lurking in the woods.

I hope the scumbags who did that to her do come so I can give them what they deserve.

She protested about taking my bed at first. But I told her I'd sleep on the couch; she has no idea I camp out outside her door.

Before she rises each morning, I roll up my blanket and move to the living room. The military taught me to sleep anywhere. The wooden cabin floor is no hardship for me. All the comfort I need is knowing that Indigo is sleeping while I'm protecting her. I just wish I knew what from.

This morning I'm making coffee when she surfaces from the bedroom, yawning daintily with her eyes groggy from sleep.

"Morning, Rainbow."

She smiles shyly at the pet name I've given her, and my heart melts a little more. She stretches like a kitten, and I'm overcome by my want to keep her. I've never had anyone who was mine before.

I grew up in foster care, and while the foster parents were good to me, no one wanted to adopt me into their family. A sullen boy with a love of firearms and a marksman's aim spells trouble wherever he goes. One look at me and people thought I was trouble, so I ended up living up to people's expectations.

I ran around with a bad crowd. We broke into a convenience store once and stole bars of chocolate.

A crime so innocent in its motivation it could make you weep. Boys wanting candy.

Too bad a cop car happened to be cruising past as we ran out with our spoils. It landed me a spell in juvie. It was there I learned about the opportunities in the military. They recruit from places like that. Giving boys a purpose in life, a chance to channel their energy into something good.

The military saved me, that's for sure. Even if it spat me out a damaged man.

When my condition got too bad and they gave me an honorable discharge, I was lost. The only family I ever had was in the military. Another guy, Kobe, our unit captain, was discharged around the same time. He grew up on the mountain, alongside some of the other guys in the unit, and convinced me to come here to Wild Heart Mountain.

I'm glad he did. The only time I ever felt like I belonged somewhere was in the military. I like my solitude, but it's comforting to know my buddies are nearby. Sure, I've been lonely at times, but for a juvenile delinquent who probably would have ended up in prison if he hadn't joined the Marines, it's not a bad life. I'm thankful every day that I am where I am and not staring at the walls of a prison cell.

I can handle the nightmares and the shakes and the dark thoughts out here alone. At least I thought I could, until Indigo wandered onto my mountain.

As I watch her yawn, stretching her arms above her head, a peace settles over me.

I'll never get tired of seeing her in my clothes, even though they're far too big on her. If she stays, I'll take her shopping just as soon as she'll let me.

"You up to a walk in the woods today? I've got some traps that need checking."

And I want to walk the perimeter of my property to make sure no one's hanging around. But I don't mention that to Indigo.

"Yeah." She slides onto the kitchen bar stool as I place a plate of scrambled eggs and thick bacon down in front of her. "Is this for me?"

"Sure is."

I like looking after Indigo. I'll cook breakfast for her every morning for the rest of my life if she'll let me.

"Thank you, Rhys."

She eats slowly, which is a good sign. After the state she was in when I found her, it's reassuring that she no longer has to scarf food as if it's her last meal.

As we're finishing eating, there's the sound of a car pulling up.

Indigo gives a frightened yelp, and her eyes go wide. She clutches me in terror, and even though she's scared, I'm glad she's clinging to me for comfort.

"It's probably just Symon."

But I grab my shotgun just in case as I go to the window. I pull the curtain back and sure enough. Symon's walking up to the front door.

"Symon's the park ranger. He's the only person who knows you're here."

"You told someone I was here?" There's panic in her voice.

"When I found you, I thought you might have been a lost hiker. You can trust Symon."

She's standing with one hand on the kitchen counter, bouncing on the balls of her feet and ready to run.

"Hey Symon."

We fist bump as I let him in, and I rest the gun beside the door.

His eyes go to Indigo, and a surge of jealousy hits my blood. Which is ridiculous. He's married and so in love with Leonie it's hard to watch them together.

"Hey," he says to Indigo. He's carrying a bag, and he slides it off his shoulder. "Leonie thought you might need these."

He slides the bag to Indigo, and she opens it tentatively. The bag's packed with clothes, and she pulls out a t-shirt and sweater and leggings. There's also a new pack of underwear and a pack of socks.

Warmth floods my heart at the kindness of my friends. Without question, Symon and his wife have provided for a stranger based only on the fact that I've taken her in.

"Thank you," Indigo and I say at the same time.

She goes to change, and I pour Symon a coffee.

"Any news?"

As ranger for Wild Heart Mountain, Symon will be the first to hear if there's anyone sketchy hanging around. But he shakes his head.

"I've made discreet inquires, but no one's looking for a girl. Hailey's working at the tourist office and will let me know if anyone suspicious comes in."

Hailey is Kobe's wife. Again, I'm thankful for my network of friends on the mountain. They're more than friends. They're my family.

Indigo comes back as we're talking. She hasn't given me any more information about her situation, but the longer she stays, the less I want to know. I couldn't stand it if I found out she was married or something.

Before Symon leaves, he scribbles his phone number on a piece of paper and sticks it to the fridge with a magnet.

"You get into any trouble out here when Rhys isn't around, you call me. Okay."

Indigo nods.

"We're family out here," he adds. "We look out for each other."

She blinks rapidly, and I think she's going to cry.

"Thank you," she whispers. The hard edges from when I first met her are gone, replaced by a vulnerable woman who needs more than shelter. She needs a home.

Symon leaves, and I spend the rest of the day with Indigo. We walk in the woods with my shotgun slung over my shoulder.

I show her my traps, and she seems genuinely interested and not queasy at all about the animals we bring back.

As we're walking, I take her hand in mine, and I don't let it go until I see the deer.

6

INDIGO

Rhys's hand in mine warms me up in a way I can't explain. It's not just the warmth of his body. It's the warmth of his soul. He might just be the first really good man I've ever met.

I'm touched by the generosity of his friends, who don't know me but are willing to help just because Rhys has taken me in. I wish I had friends like that.

The last few days I've been focused on my recovery, but now I have to think about my next step. I have nowhere to go and no money.

Rhys says I can stay as long as I need, but what if I want to stay forever? The longer I spend with this man, the stronger my feelings for him grow. He's thoughtful and gentle and kind, not to mention muscular and hot.

With his hand in mine, I let myself dream of a future together where I'm safe in his cabin forever.

Rhys stops abruptly and puts a hand up to his lips, indicating for me to be silent. I follow his gaze, and up ahead behind a low bush is a deer. Her head is dipped as she drinks from a pool of water collected at the bottom of the slope below us.

Rhys drops my hand and slides the rifle off his back. I step out of his way and wince at the crunching sound underfoot. He shoots me a look, silently telling me to stay where I am.

He moves silently and gracefully for a big man, stealthily raising the rifle to his cheek as he maneuvers into position.

My heart is thumping in my chest. I've never been on a hunt before, and the thought that we might be catching dinner has me excited. It's so primal, tapping into our most basic instincts to survive.

But as I watch Rhys flick off the safety, I realize something's not right. A tremor runs through his hands. He keeps focused down the sight of the gun, but the trembling gets so bad that his finger jerks against the trigger.

He takes the shot and it goes wide, tearing through a branch above the deer's head. She takes off into the forest, the opportunity missed.

Rhys is muttering curses as he lowers the rifle, and he won't look me in the eye.

He slides the rifle over his shoulder and shoves his hands in his pockets.

"Come on. I want to check the other traps."

He doesn't want to talk about it, and I respect that. I'm not the only one keeping secrets.

Screams wake me in the night, the sound of a man yelling right outside my door. I tear out of bed and pull the door open and almost trip over Rhys. He's lying on the floor with a cushion from the couch as a pillow and a blanket over him. By his side is his rifle.

His eyes are closed, and he's thrashing wildly. He moans, and the sound is so guttural it sounds like a dying animal.

"Rhys." I push the rifle away with my foot in case he freaks out and grabs it.

"Rhys." This time I say it louder and give him a shake, trying to wake him up. "You're having a bad dream."

He pushes against me but I crouch next to him, taking his broad shoulders in my hands.

"Rhys, wake up!" His eyes fly open and he looks around wildly, his pupils like saucers.

"It's me, Indigo."

His gaze settles on my face, and he sucks in large breaths as his pupils return to normal. Beads of sweat pool on his forehead and I wipe them away with the back of my hand, smoothing his hair back.

"You were having a nightmare."

He doesn't speak, and it's the first time I've seen him vulnerable.

"I'll get you a glass of water." I go to stand up to give him some time to compose himself, but he rises onto his elbows and reaches for me.

"No. Stay here."

I crouch back down, and he sits up and leans into me. My arms wrap around him, and I pull his head to my chest. My hand runs down his back, soothing him as I rock gently. It's how my mom used to hold me when I woke up with night terrors.

"Were you sleeping on the floor?"

He pulls his head back, and his eyes are deep pools in the dim light. "I was making sure no one can get to you."

He says it so matter-of-factly, but the gesture touches me. That he would sleep outside my door, like a guard. "I thought you were sleeping on the couch."

"I'm protecting you."

My heart opens to this man. Damaged in his own way, protecting a damaged girl. But I can't let him sleep on the hard floor.

"You're not sleeping on the floor."

I sit back, releasing him, and he gets up and gathers his cushion and blanket.

"You can put me back on the couch, but I won't stay there. You're mine to protect, Indigo…"

"You're not sleeping on the couch or the floor." I push open the bedroom door. "You're sharing the bed with me."

He hesitates, and my heart climbs into my throat. Maybe I've been too forward. Maybe I've misinterpreted the signs.

"Are you sure?"

"Yes." I take his hand. "I'm not leaving you out here alone, Rhys."

He follows me into the bedroom, and we climb into bed together. Rhys takes the left hand side, putting himself between me and the door.

I mean to keep my distance, but with Rhys beside me I can't. We get in on opposite sides of the bed, but we find each other in the middle.

His arm drapes over my hip, and my body molds to his. It's as if we're made for this, as if we've done this a hundred times.

I lie in the darkness enjoying the heat from his body, but questions run through my mind.

"Do you often have nightmares?"

For a long time Rhys doesn't say anything, and I

think he's fallen asleep. Then he speaks. "Ever since my first kill."

The words send a chill through me and I press myself against him, needing the warmth. He doesn't say more, and soon his breathing deepens with sleep.

I lie awake for a long time wondering what causes a man to scream in the night.

7

INDIGO

I wake the next morning with a hard rod pressed into my lower back and damp heat between my legs. A smile spreads across my lips when I realize what it is that's prodding my back.

With the sun streaming through the window, it's easy to forget Rhys's nightmare. And right now, his hardness behind me feels too good.

I move my hips against him, and my smile broadens when he stirs. He pushes against me, and I roll my hips back toward him.

I'm facing the wall and I can't see him, but I'm aware of every inch of his body. I'm aware of his hand as it moves from my hips, over the curves of my stomach, and up to my breasts. The way my nipples pebble as he caresses them through my t-shirt. Then, when his hand slides under my shirt so there's nothing between us, the moan that escapes my lips and the way my back arches into him.

Then his lips are on the back of my neck, the heat from his mouth sending shivers down my spine.

We don't talk. I'm too afraid to break the spell. I let his hands rove over my body as I tilt my hips and rub against his hardness.

There's an ache in my core that's been growing with every day that we spend together. A needy tug, and I'm ready for release.

His hand slides between my legs, and I moan as he rubs me through my panties. They're already drenched, and he pulls the fabric aside to stroke my soaking folds.

A small cry escapes me. There's something intense and secretive about not speaking. But I'm sure as hell going to moan when he makes me feel this good.

My hand reaches behind until I find his length. Rhys is only in his underwear, and I slide my hand inside the fabric to pop his cock out. My fingers barely fit around his girth, it's that big.

At the same time, his finger slides into me, and I jerk backwards at the sudden sensation. I've never been with a man before, and the things I'm feeling are all new.

His palm rubs against my most sensitive spot while his finger slides into my pussy.

I'm stroking his dick at the same time, my movements getting more jerky as the pleasure overtakes me.

I push my ass back into him. My panties form a barrier between us, and they're soaked through from his pre-cum and my arousal.

I want to rip my panties off and slide onto his cock. But I'm too close to coming on his hand. His palm moves in little circles, and I can't bear it any longer. My pants turn to cries as my orgasm hits. I clench his fingers as my pussy convulses, and I tug hard on his cock with my hand. He groans and hot liquid squirts up my back.

It's so dirty and hot that I come again, riding his palm while my body shakes.

When we're both finished, the only sound is our hard breathing. Only then do I turn to face Rhys. He's got a big grin on his face.

"Morning, Rainbow."

I like the nickname he's given me. It's sounds hopeful and pretty. Two things I definitely wasn't when I arrived here, but am starting to feel whenever I'm around Rhys.

"That was…"

I'm not sure how to describe it. Amazing, wonderful…

"…the release I needed."

I regret the words as soon as I've said them. They

sound hollow and ungrateful, as if it didn't mean anything when it meant the world to me.

The grin falls from his face. He pulls up his pants and slides out of bed.

"Glad I could be of service." There's a hard note to his voice that I haven't heard before.

"I didn't mean it like that…"

I sit up in bed, but he's already pulling his t-shirt on. "It's okay, Indigo."

But it's not okay. The only man who's ever been nice to me, and he thinks I'm using him. But aren't I? I'm sleeping in his bed, eating his food, using his hot water, all the while not telling him anything about myself. Perhaps it's time to come clean.

8

INDIGO

The next few days are the happiest of my life. During the day, we wander Rhys's property, checking his traps and processing any animals he catches. We see the deer again, but he lets it go by without raising his gun.

Instead, we pull rabbits out of traps, and he teaches me how to skin them in such a way as to leave the pelt intact. He sells the pelts in town as well as any spare meat.

Conversation flows easily, skirting around the topics neither of us want to talk about.

My black eye fades, and I grow stronger every day. But I don't talk about leaving. I don't know where I'll go. I'm so happy here.

The days are good, but the nights, oh Lord, the

nights. Every night Rhys climbs into bed beside me, and we rub against each other until we come.

Our hands and bodies have been busy exploring each other. We haven't had proper sex yet, and my need for him is growing every day. Rhys doesn't make any moves to take it further, and I worry that he doesn't want to. But his hard cock tells a different story.

He's hard for me when he wakes up and we rub against each other like we did the first day. But every time I try to guide his dick to my opening, he pulls back.

I guess he has his reasons. But it's killing me.

When we've both come, he gets out of bed and into the shower. There's intimacy between us yet also a distance, like he's holding back.

Maybe this is the tradeoff for keeping secrets. Perhaps there can be no real intimacy until we show each other our darkness.

We're lying in bed that night facing each other. Rhys insists on sleeping on the side where the door is, and he keeps his gun next to him on the floor. I'm touched by his protectiveness. I've never been cared for before.

His hands slide down my body, and his mouth closes over mine. In just a week his touch has become so familiar. I sigh contentedly as his lips move across my neck, finding the erogenous zone behind my ear.

My panties are already soaking by the time his hand slides over them.

Rhys isn't much of a talker during sexy times, but I understand by the groan that comes out of his lips that he's enjoying my body.

One of my hands wraps around his cock and I slide it slowly down his shaft the way that he likes. My fingernails on the other hand scrape along his balls, and he lets out a hiss at the sensation.

Then his finger is inside me, and I'm lost in my own pleasure. My movements on his cock get faster, more erratic as my own pleasure builds. I press into his palm, grinding myself against him as I search for a release.

I'm using both hands on his cock now, and it's slick with pre-cum. There're high-pitched panting noises coming from my throat, and I don't recognize them as myself. Then I'm coming, my pussy clenching on his fingers. I give a hard tug on his cock and his cum squirts out, pouring over my fingers and coating my belly in his sweet stickiness.

We stare at each other in the light of the bedside lamp, panting hard from what we've just done.

We've gotten each other off like this for the last few nights and I love it, but I want more.

Rhys gets out of bed and returns with a warm

flannel. He wipes down my stomach, planting gentle kisses on my skin as he mops up the sticky mess.

He cares for me. In this moment, I'm sure that he does.

"Rhys…" He cuts me off with a kiss on the lips. If I didn't know better, I'd think he didn't want me to talk.

I pull back because I want to talk. I'm ready to talk.

"My real name isn't Indigo."

I say it in a rush before he can stop me. Rhys doesn't say anything, and I rush on while I'm feeling brave.

"I ran away from The Seekers of Light." Recognition flicks across his face. "Do you know it?"

"It's that cult at the base of Blue Ridge, isn't it?"

I glance down, not able to meet his eye. I'm embarrassed that I ended up in a place like that. I didn't even realize it was a cult when I joined, which shows how stupid I was.

"Yeah. They call it a compound. It seemed like a refuge for a person like me."

He tilts my chin up.

"And what kind of person is that?"

He says it kindly. Rhys thinks I'm a good person, but he's only known me for a week. A week where I've lived in an alternate world. When he found me, I could be whoever I wanted to be. I could be someone good. And that's what I've been doing, only showing him the best parts of myself. But I haven't always been a good person.

"When I joined the Seekers, I'd just come out of a juvie center."

I glance up at Rhys, expecting him to be horrified or disappointed. But he's looking at me with the same steady gaze as if it's nothing to find out the woman he's been sharing a bed with was a juvenile delinquent.

"And the cult felt like a fresh start?"

He hasn't asked me what I went in for. What I did that got me sent to juvie.

"Don't you want to know what I did?"

He takes a strand of hair and curls it behind my ear.

"You can tell me if you want. But your past doesn't define you, Indigo."

It takes a moment to realize what he's saying. All my life my past *has* defined me. People have made judgements about me, the daughter of a junkie. Then, when they finally took me from my mother, a foster child too old to be adopted, passed through the system as just another troubled teenage girl. When I was caught stealing vapes, it was easy to send me to the center. I was just another kid heading down the wrong path.

When I came out, I swore I wouldn't go back to

detention. The Seekers of Light seemed like some-where I could keep out of trouble, somewhere to belong.

I tell Rhys all of this, and he listens quietly.

"Let me guess. The cult welcomed you in and told you it was the fresh start you needed?"

There's an edge to his voice, and he pulls the flannel tight between his fingers.

"Something like that."

"They prey on vulnerable people, Indigo. People who are searching for something and don't know what that is."

I hate that I fell prey to them, I was so naive to believe their talk about redemption.

"And they did this to you?" His fingertips brush over the skin around my eye where the bruising is almost faded. I wince even though his touch is gentle.

I'm ashamed that I let this happen to me. I'm ashamed that it wasn't the first time. My gaze dips, and Rhys pulls me toward him. His arms wrap around me in a comforting embrace. My cheek rests against his chest, and the steady beat of his heart gives me the courage to go on. I'm baring myself to him and I want him to know it all, to know all my flaws and mistakes and vulnerabilities.

I begin to talk, telling him everything about The Seekers of Light.

I thought I'd found somewhere to belong at the compound, but I was stupid and naive and vulnerable. They took me in, and at first it was fine. A bed to sleep in and a community to be a part of. But then the punishments started. If I looked at one of the men the wrong way or didn't peel the potatoes quickly enough, I'd spend the night in the pigsty sleeping with the animals.

I see what they were doing. They were trying to break my spirit. Wear me down so I would comply with their wishes like the other women.

The first time the leader came to get me from the pigsty to spend the night in his room, I refused. That's how I got the black eye.

He didn't force me, but I knew it wouldn't be long before I was beaten so much, I'd have to comply.

I ran that night.

When I finish telling my story, Rhys's heartbeat is going a mile a minute and his body is still. I try to pull back, but he keeps his arms locked around me.

"Tell me more about the compound."

His voice is calm and doesn't betray any of the anger that I can tell he's feeling. Maybe he's trying to calm me down, because he asks a lot of questions. And it is soothing describing the routines and stupid outfits the leaders wear. I haven't talked about this before, and it helps to get it all out.

"I don't know if they're looking for me or not, but I don't want to go back."

"You never have to go back. Those people will never hurt you again, Rainbow. Never again."

I want to believe his words, and in the comfort of his bed with his arms around me, I can almost believe it's true.

He wraps his arms tight around me. He's gone quiet, but I don't hear him fall asleep. I guess it's a lot to take in. But I'm glad I told him, that I'm not carrying that burden anymore.

With my conscience clear, eventually I fall asleep.

9

RHYS

 don't sleep after Indigo's confession. There's too much rage coursing through my body. She's been hurt by scumbags who prey on the vulnerable. By some asshole setting himself up as a community leader and taking advantage of women.

Scum like that don't deserve to live.

I lie as still as I can, keeping my breathing even until Indigo falls asleep. But I don't sleep. My mind is busy planning how I'm going to take this asshole out.

I quizzed her about the compound, showing interest but being careful not to draw her attention to my real motive. Now I go over everything she told me: the location of the hole in the fence she crawled through, the buildings on the edge of the compound, the dawn ceremony facing the sun led by the man wearing a blue cloak.

The military taught me to sleep anywhere, and it also taught me to stay awake. I wait until a couple of hours before dawn before slipping out of bed.

I move quietly, as I was trained to do. Indigo sleeps on her side, one arm thrown over the blankets and her mouth slack with sleep.

She's come to mean so much to me in this week that we've spent together. When our bodies move together in bed, my very soul lifts.

But she made it clear that I'm just a release for her, part of the healing process as she gathers her strength to move on. Which is why I haven't gone further with her. I can't bear the thought of claiming her if she's not really mine.

I wish it wasn't true. I wish she could stay here forever, but I get why she would want to move on. I've been somewhere for her to gather her strength, recover and gain confidence. Why would she want to stay with an old vet who has night terrors and shaky hands?

But even if I don't mean as much to Indigo as she does to me, I can give her this. I can give her her revenge.

I grab my long range rifle and my camouflage gear.

It's time to hunt.

It's a forty minute drive to the Blue Ridge Mountain range on the other side of Wild Heart Mountain. It's still dark when I park on the narrow country lane that borders the compound.

I find the hole in the fence exactly where she said it was. It's a small hole, and I use wire cutters to widen it enough to get through with my gear.

I don't care that I leave behind a great big gaping hole in the fence, I don't care who finds me. I only care about taking out the assholes that hurt Indigo.

Thin woodland runs alongside the fence, and I move stealthily though the trees until I get to the edge of the forest. I crouch in the bushes looking out on the clearing. It's about a hundred meters to the first building.

The first grey light tinges the sky. There's no one around, but from what Indigo told me, it won't be long until they come out for dawn prayers.

Keeping low to the ground, I make a dash for the white brick building that is closest. Snuffling noises come from inside as I climb up the drainpipe and onto the roof. It's the pigsty, and I hope like hell no poor soul is sleeping there tonight. A flash of anger spikes through me at the thought of Indigo being made to sleep in a pigsty. I push it down. There's no room for emotion. I need to focus.

Once on the roof, I press my body flat and belly-crawl to the edge of the building.

In the center of the clearing is a concrete square with a podium facing east. That's where the leader will stand. I slide my rifle out of the case, line up the site, and wait.

As the sky lightens to ash grey, there's movement from the other buildings. Women and men shuffle out into the cold dawn day. They're wearing red cloaks like the one I found Indigo in. They don't talk but move silently to the square.

From another building comes a group of men. My heart rate jumps a notch when I see the man in a blue robe. My target.

I take deep breaths to slow my pulse and find him in the crosshairs as he ascends the podium.

The rifle butts against my cheek and I click off the safety, ready to take my vengeance. This man hurt my girl, and he will pay. For the first time since I've been back, my hand doesn't shake when I hold a gun.

It might be anger giving me focus or the love I have for Indigo, but my finger is steady as I put it to the trigger.

10

INDIGO

I stir in the night and roll over to snuggle into Rhys, but his side of the bed is empty. Not just empty. It's cold.

"Rhys?" I sit up and check the bedside clock. It's five-twenty a.m. Too early to be up. But based on the way the covers are pulled up on his side of the bed, it's clear he's been gone for a while.

"Rhys," I call louder this time as I slip out of bed. He's not in the bathroom, so I pad out of the room.

But the cabin's empty.

An uneasy feeling pools in my gut. Rhys hasn't left my side since I got here. He may have gone trapping or hunting early, but he would have told me. I'm sure.

That's when I see the note on the kitchen counter, and I snatch it up.

· · ·

No one will hurt you again.
    Back soon.
    Rhys.

I stare at the note in horror.

No one will hurt you again.

My eyes dart to the gun rack on the wall. There's one missing. It's the long range rifle from the top rack, the one he takes when we go hunting.

My stomach drops as realization sets in. He's gone to the compound. I told him who hurt me, and now he's going to make them pay.

With my heart hammering in my chest, I grab the phone number that Symon left on the fridge. It's not yet six a.m., but I can't let Rhys do this for me.

Symon picks up on the second ring, his voice groggy from sleep.

"It's Indigo. I need your help."

It's too much to explain on the phone, but Symon promises to come without question. I dress quickly and pace the front porch until his pickup arrives.

On the drive down the mountain, I explain about the cult and what I think Rhys is going to do.

I was embarrassed to tell anyone about my past, but now I've told two people in less than twelve hours. Symon takes in my story without judgment, and I feel a wave of affection for him. Not the same way I feel about Rhys, but as if we could be friends.

"I think Rhys is going to do something stupid. He took the long range rifle."

Symon swears under his breath and pumps the accelerator.

"Do you think he has it in him to…to…shoot someone?"

Symon gives me an odd look. "You do know what he did in the military, right?"

Dread grips my heart. "I know he was a Marine."

"He was a Scout Sniper, a trained HOG."

"HOG?" I grip the handle above the door, feeling faint.

"Hunter of Gunmen. I've never met anyone as good a shot as Rhys. He never missed once."

The words thunder in my brain. He was a sniper. He killed people for a living. Murder sanctioned by the government. No wonder he shakes. No wonder he has nightmares.

My heart goes out to Rhys. All this time he's been looking after me, but I should have been looking after him. Now he's going to shoot someone and get himself put in prison all because of me.

"Go faster."

We tear down the mountain, bumping over potholes until we get to the lane where I made my escape. Rhys's pickup is parked in the lane, and we screech to a halt next to it as the first light tinges the sky.

I'm out the door before Symon has the engine off.

"Hey," he hisses. "You can't go in there alone."

But I'm already halfway through the fence. It's pushed open wider than when I left it, which means Rhys has already gone through.

I dash through the woods, not caring about the noise I make. I hear Symon crashing behind me. It's only when we come to the clearing that I stop.

Residents are emerging from the sleeping quarters. They're wearing the red cloaks we all had to wear when outside. Memories flood my brain, and my feet are like lead. Being back in this place makes my pulse race and my stomach roil.

I try to move my feet, but I don't think I can go on. I'm hyperventilating when Symon grabs my arm and turns me to face him.

"You're okay, Indigo. They can't hurt you now."

His reassurance gives me the strength I need.

Symon spots Rhys first, lying flat atop the pigsty.

You wouldn't know there was a man there if you weren't looking for him.

"There he is."

We skirt around the clearing until we can make a dash without being seen. If they catch us in here, there's no telling what they'll do. The Seekers of Light have their own weapons stash and enough brainwashed acolytes who will do anything the leader asks. It's a dangerous situation.

We get to the back of the building, and Symon gives me a leg up to the roof.

"I'll be lookout," he whispers.

I climb over the ledge, keeping low, and scramble to where Rhys is. The leader is almost at the podium and Rhys is dead still, his finger poised on the trigger. There's no shaking now, only a complete and deadly focus.

The leader reaches the podium, and Rhys's finger moves.

"Stop," I hiss as I grab him by the ankle.

Rhys spins around, his face focused and hard, unrecognizable.

"What are you doing here, Indigo?"

"I'm stopping you from doing something stupid." I crawl on my belly up to him, keeping my voice low so it doesn't carry across the clearing. "We need to go."

His face softens and he brushes my cheek, but the hardness doesn't leave his eyes.

"I need to get justice for you, Rainbow. Go. Take my keys and drive as far away from this as you can. It will all be over soon."

He hands me his car keys from his pocket, but I don't take them. He really means to go through with this, and I'm not sure I can stop him.

He turns back to his gun, and I pull on his shoulder. "No. Rhys, don't do this."

My voice is panicked, and I'm trying to keep it low, but I'm desperate. I've never seen him like this, and it's frightening.

"I don't need justice, Rhys. Come home with me."

"They hurt you, Indigo. I love you, and I'll hurt anyone who harms you. I'll do anything for you. Don't you know that?"

He turns back to the rifle and shuffles it into position.

"Live. That's what you can do for me." He pauses and I go on, hoping I've got his attention. "I've finally found a place where I belong, and that's with you, Rhys. I can't have you going away to prison. Not when I've just found you. Don't do that to me."

He pauses and lowers the rifle. This time when he looks at me, it's with a softer expression.

"You want to stay with me?"

"Yes, of course I do. It's the only real home I've ever had because you're in it. Come home with me."

My cheeks are wet with tears, and I'm trying to sob quietly. He rests the rifle on the roof and belly-slides backwards to wipe the tears from my cheeks.

"I thought you wanted to leave, to move on."

"Are you crazy? I want to be wherever you are. I love you, Rhys."

"But I am kind of crazy. I'm a broken man. I have PTSD. That's why my hands shake and why I have nightmares. Are you sure you want that baggage?"

I almost laugh out loud. "Please, I can hardly complain about baggage. For a long time, I thought I was broken, but with you, I feel whole. I finally have somewhere I belong."

He cups my cheeks in his hands.

"You'll always have a home with me."

His lips press to mine, and I kiss him back passionately. There's a scuffling sound from behind us. Rhys turns quickly and ducks my head down as he whips out a handgun from his waist.

"You two want to wrap it up. I'd like to get out of here before the singing starts."

Symon's peering at us from over the ledge. Rhys lowers his gun, a surprised expression on his face.

"What are you doing here?"

"Saving your sorry ass."

Rhys breaks into a grin. "Let's get the fuck out of here. This place gives me the creeps."

We slide down the drain pipe the same way we got up. Any sounds we make are hidden by the hymns coming from the congregation.

We're about to dash for the woods when Rhys squeezes my hand. "Wait for me in the car."

Before I can protest, he slinks around the corner and out of sight. I give Symon a wild look, but he pushes me forward.

"Come on, let's get you out of here. Rhys can look after himself."

We're almost at the fence when I hear a commotion behind us. Rhys comes crashing through the bush carrying something in his arms.

"Run," he says, but he's laughing.

There're screams from the compound and snorting noises. We push through the fence and race to the pickups. It's only when I get in that I see what he's got in his arms.

"Hold this." He pushes two pink squirming bundles at me. "I always wanted pigs at the cabin."

I take the piglets he thrusts at me.

"What did you do?"

"I let the pigs out. Couldn't resist."

We're laughing as we head back to Wild Heart Mountain with Symon following in his pickup.

11

RHYS

It's a few hours later, and Symon has just left my cabin after having a cooked breakfast. It was the least I could do for him after coming out to help Indigo without hesitation.

I see him off on the porch, and we give each other a bro hug. He's more like a brother to me, and I promise to have him and Leonie over for dinner soon. I can't wait for Indigo to meet everyone, and I'm sure she'll love the other girls.

The pigs are settled in a makeshift pen that I hastily put together with a few spare logs. I'll build a proper pen for them tomorrow. But today, I want to spend time with my girl.

Indigo is sitting on the couch nursing a cup of coffee when I come in from seeing off Symon. I'm struck by her beauty as the light falls on her hair, showing off the various shades of caramel.

Her eye is completely healed, her cheeks round and rosy as she smiles at me. I'm filled with love for her and a sense of wonder. I thought I was protecting her, but she was protecting me. Protecting me from myself. There will always be a darkness inside me, but she's awoken a gentleness in me too.

"Come here." I hold out my hand, and she stands from the couch.

"Where are we going?" I take the almost empty coffee mug out of her hand and place it on the kitchen counter as I lead her to the bedroom.

"It's time to make you mine properly."

I didn't want to take her until I knew it was for keeps. I didn't want to complicate things or give Indigo anything else to worry about. So I held myself back as much as I could. She was too damn hard to resist. But now there's no reason to hold back.

Indigo has agreed to stay here, to change her name officially to Indigo so no one can find her. And she'll take my last name soon. She just doesn't know it yet.

I won't ask her yet. One step at time. For now, it's enough to claim her as my woman, the way I've been aching to do ever since I carried her to my cabin.

Before we reach the bedroom, I scoop her into my arms. Indigo gives a shriek as I carry her over the threshold of the bedroom.

"What are you doing?" She giggles as I drop her onto the bed.

"This is *our* bedroom now. Everything in this cabin is as much yours as mine now. You understand?"

Indigo gets up on her knees and scoots over to the side of the bed. She gives me a wicked look as her hands reach for my belt buckle.

"Does that include your cock?"

I love the sound of the dirty word on her lips and my dick twitches in my pants, practically nodding its head at her.

"Rainbow, my cock is yours to do with what you want."

"I like the sound of that."

Her hands make quick work of the belt, and she's soon got my cock in her hands. I want to push her down on the bed, but it's important she has control here. I want her to feel safe. I want her to know everything we do here is her decision.

Still, it's a surprise when she dips her head and presses her lips to my tip.

I hiss in a breath as her warm mouth takes me in. Her hands grip my shaft as her mouth moves clumsily over my cock.

"You ever done this before?"

She slides me out of her mouth. "Am I doing something wrong?"

"No, Rainbow, you're doing everything right."

With a content smile, she parts her lips and slips me back into her mouth. The sensation is too fucking good. My hands tangle in her hair and I pump my hips, needing to go deeper. My girl opens her mouth wide, gagging as my cock bumps up against the back of her throat.

"Tilt your head back and slack your jaw."

She does as she's told, opening her throat wide as I plunge in deep.

"That's it, good girl."

Her eyes light up at the praise and she moans, sending vibrations up my cock. The top of her blouse is open and her tits bounce up and down, two soft globes that I'm dying to get my hands on.

It feels sensational to be in her mouth, but this isn't where I want to come. I want to pleasure my woman and send my seed shooting into her belly.

Gently, I pull back, letting my dick slide out of her mouth with a pop. She looks disappointed.

"I want to be inside you, Indigo."

My fingers pull at her buttons. She helps me as they begin to shake. At first, I was embarrassed about my PTSD and the trembling it sets off. But

Indigo doesn't seem to care. She sees me for who I am, not for what I lack.

It doesn't take long to shed our clothes, and then she's lying on the bed before me with her knees bent. I pull her thighs apart, opening up her pink pussy that my hand has gotten to know so well over the past week.

She bites her lip and lifts her head to look me in the eye.

"I've never done this before, Rhys. I've never gone all the way."

I suspected as much from how tight her pussy was, but the confession makes my dick sing. I'll be the first and only man to claim this woman. No one will ever be here. Indigo is all mine.

"It's okay, honey. I got you."

My head dips between her legs, and I feast on her sweet cunt. Her scent is heady and her taste musky and sweet. It's the best fucking meal I've ever tasted.

Indigo writhes under me, moaning my name as softly as the whisper of the trees in the forest. Her pussy grips my fingers, and a gush of wetness coats my tongue. With her orgasm soaring through her body, I come onto my knees and line my dick up with her opening.

"I don't want there to be anything between us, Indigo. I'm clean."

She sits up on her elbows. "I'm not on birth control."

My cock is circling her entrance, and it twitches as her words.

"Honey, the sooner I get my baby in your belly, the better. I want to make little rainbows; I want a family with you. Kids to love and take care of the way we never were."

She lets out a sob, and I pull back. "What is it? What's wrong?"

"I want all that too, Rhys. I was worried you didn't."

"Honey, I want it all with you. Every part of you, everything you've got to give."

We gaze at each other a long time, my dick resting at her opening as our gazes lock on each other. Our souls are exposed and we're at our most vulnerable, yet there's nothing but love between us.

"You're gonna need a bigger cabin."

My hand clasps the back of her head, and we smile at each other. I keep my eyes on her as I slide inside. She winces when I reach her virgin barrier, and she pinches her eyes closed.

"Eyes on me, Indigo. Eyes on me."

Her pussy is squeezing my cock, but I'm not stopping until I've claimed her. I thrust hard, hitting the bullseye and pushing through her barrier.

Her eyes widen, but she holds the pain inside.

Neither of us move, panting together as our bodies adjust to one another.

Her pussy is like a vice, and when the pressure eases, only then do I move. Slowly I slide out and back in, keeping my movements slow and small. Her pussy tugs my cock, and I could get lost inside her. But I've been trained to keep control and this is what I do, putting my needs aside until her face goes slack and moans of pleasure escape her lips.

"Rhys," she whines. "It feels too good."

Only then, as she rolls her hips looking for a release, do I let myself get lost in her. I give up control and get carried away in the moment, carried away with Indigo and the way our bodies move together.

All our pain and all our pasts come together and evaporate as our bodies join. My soul soars, and there's nothing in the world but this moment. Whatever we did in the past, our slates are wiped clean. It's just me and my woman in this moment, the physical connection joining our souls in a way that can't be undone.

Her back arches as her pussy clenches. I've never seen anything as sexy as Indigo coming underneath me. I explode with her, shooting hot cum straight into her womb. Giving her everything I've got and hoping it's enough. My hips pump, and just as I think we're done, she wiggles against me again.

Another orgasm claims her, sucking my cum further into her body. I hope it reaches its mark. I hope my shot is straight and true.

I want to make a family with this woman, and I can't wait to start.

EPILOGUE

INDIGO

Six months later…

Rhys moves gracefully for a man who lives up a mountain. I guess it's his stealth as a hunter that also makes him an excellent ballroom dancer.

It was his idea to do a traditional first dance. Frank Sinatra croons out of the speakers as Rhys twirls me around the dance floor.

We practiced the moves in the cabin, me tripping over his feet while he nimbly sprang out of the way.

Our guests watch from the edges of the temporary dance floor that's been set down at Angie's bar. It was a small ceremony. The only family either of us have is right here on the mountain.

Over the past six months, I've been taken in by

Rhys's former Marine pals and their wives. The guys get together once a month, but the women are more social. We meet up every week, and someone's always having one couple or another over for dinner. Rhys grumbles that he's lost his recluse status, but I know he doesn't really mind. If I'm happy, he's happy. And these days, I'm happy all the time.

The dance ends, and I twirl into Rhys's arms. We're both out of breath and we gaze at each other, panting slightly.

Rhys has a wide grin on his face, and mine must be just as goofy.

"I love you, wife."

"I love you too, husband."

I giggle, still getting used to being someone's wife.

Other couples join us on the dance floor, and Rhys leans in until his breath tickles my neck.

"You look sexy tonight, Rainbow."

His hand slides down the back of my satin dress to rest on the curve of my rump. There's instant heat between my legs as I brush up against him.

"Come on."

He grabs my hand and leads me off the dance floor.

"Where are we going?"

"To consummate this marriage."

I giggle as he leads me to a door by the side of the bar that says 'staff only.' Rhys glances around the room to check that no one's watching.

"Are we going to consummate this marriage in a broom closet?"

Rhys growls as he pushes the door open.

"Maybe."

There's a corridor with two doors leading off it. One of them is Angie's office and the other is the supply cupboard. We don't make it past the first door before Rhys pushes me against the wall. The tension that's been keeping my body coiled ever since I saw how hot my man looks in a tux comes out in a passionate kiss. His hand slides under my dress as I lift my thigh, sliding it around him.

It was meant to just be a kiss, but things are getting heated pretty quickly.

The noise of the party is muffled behind the door, and there's a window that means anyone looking in could see us.

"Come here."

Rhys takes my hand, and we stumble down the corridor to the door at the end. We're kissing as Rhys pushes it open with his hip, so we don't see the couple already in there until they jump apart.

I gasp in surprise at the sight of Angie. She's wiping her mouth, which is swollen from kissing, her lipstick smudged.

"It's not what it looks like," Angie says hastily. "We're out of napkins, and Corbin was helping me..."

"What the fuck?" Rhys says.

Angie pushes past us. "I need to get back to the party."

Corbin goes to follow her, and Rhys slaps a hand on his shoulder. "What the actual fuck, man?"

Guilt spreads over Corbin's face.

"It's not what it looks like. Don't tell the other guys, please."

He looks so guilty and pleading that Rhys nods and drops his hand.

Corbin and Angie leave, and the door swings shut behind them.

I turn to Rhys, and there's anger in his eyes. "Wasn't Corbin friends with Angie's husband?"

"Yeah," Rhys replies with a hard tone. "Paul was in our unit. He was a good guy and Corbin's best friend."

"Oh." It falls into place now, their guilty look and Rhys cold reaction.

Oh shit.

* * *

CHERISHED BY THE MOUNTAIN MAN

She's my best friend's widow and the only woman I've ever loved...

Paul was my best friend, my brother in arms, and the only one of us who didn't come back alive.

I promised that if something ever happened to him I'd look after Angie, his wife.

He's unaware that I've loved Angie for almost as long as he has.

Now she's a single mom who's running a business on her own. I sense her loneliness; I sense her need.

Angie's off-limits, but my heart beats for her. And I don't know how much longer I can resist this pull between us...

Cherished by the Mountain Man is a best friend's widow forbidden love romance featuring an ex-military mountain man and the curvy single mom he cherishes.

Corbin

The industrial dishwasher hums behind me as I wipe down the bar one last time. I've swept the floor, and the tables are wiped and reset for dinner. Only one group of tourists remain, drinking craft beer as they admire the mountain. Why the hell they aren't on the mountain on a crisp spring day like today instead of spending their afternoon drinking, I'll never know. But I should be thankful; it's thirsty tourists like these that keep Angie's Bar running.

I glance at the clock, and it's after three. The kitchen is closed for the afternoon while the chef preps for the evening shift and tidies up out back.

Angie and the kids will arrive soon. I do a last

check that everything's clean and tidy for her so she doesn't have any additional stress.

The door bursts open, bringing a blast of fresh air with it as Fran runs to the bar.

"You're lying, Jamie. That was so my pencil case."

The tourists in the corner glance up at the sudden intrusion of school children.

Fran stomps across the bar to a booth in the family area with her arms folded and a scowl on her face.

"Don't be such a baby." Her brother saunters in, all gangly pre-adolescent arms and dark hair, the mirror image of his father at that age apart from the frown on his face. Paul was always smiling. He was always cheerful, and it breaks my heart to see his son so sullen.

A pang of guilt pierces my chest.

Give them a happy life.

Paul's final words haunt my thoughts as I watch the siblings' argument play out.

Angie comes in a few moments later, her arms laden with shopping bags. There're lines around her eyes and a permanent crease between her eyebrows that I long to smooth out. Her blonde hair is tied back in a practical ponytail, and I'm itching to untie it and let her locks flow freely the way she wore her hair when we were younger.

But we're not young now.

Being a single mom, a widow, and a business owner has taken its toll on Angie. Her shoulders are hunched more than they should be and her blue eyes carry a worried look, but she's still as gorgeous as the moment I first laid eyes on her.

Angie still makes my heart thunder in my chest every time she walks into the room.

I rush to take the shopping bags off her, and she gives me a grateful smile. My heart melts at the way she looks up at me.

"Thanks, Corbin."

Her eyes briefly sparkle before a shout from across the room draws her attention to the kids.

She strides across to the booth where they've dumped their school bags. I can't hear what she's saying, but based on the gestures and low tone of her voice, they're getting one hell of a telling off. By the time she's finished, the kids are both sitting in the booth quietly with their homework in front of them.

The tourists are staring, and Angie gives them a friendly smile as she crosses the room.

"Welcome to Wild Heart Mountain. You enjoying your stay?"

She enters into a brief conversation with the customers while I take the supplies out back. I hand the bags over to Miguel the chef and help him put the food away.

When I return to the bar, Angie has brought more bags from the car.

"I'm just gonna run these upstairs, Corbin, and then I'll come back and take over."

"Take your time, Angie. Make yourself a coffee and relax. I've got this."

She gives me a grateful smile. "Thank you so much for stepping in."

One of her bar staff called in sick, and I offered to step in and do the shift.

"No problem. Indigo stopped by to go over the catering plans for the wedding."

One of my former Marine buddies is getting married this weekend, and Angie offered to host the reception here.

She cringes. "I was supposed to meet her, wasn't I? Damn, I knew there was something I'd forgotten today."

"It's fine. Miguel and I sat down with her, and it's all sorted. She's decided on the menu, and Miguel's put in the orders in town."

Angie gives a relieved sigh.

"You've a life saver, Corbin. I don't know what I'd do without you."

I've been helping Angie out at the bar ever since I came back from the military. I promised Paul I'd look after his wife and kids, and that's what I've been trying to do.

The hardest part is keeping my feelings for Angie from showing. I've spent so many years with my heart tucked up and hurting that the pain has become part of how I live.

One of the group of tourists comes up for another round, and we chat about their plans while I pour the drinks. The man is rosy cheeked, and he gushes about the beauty of this place.

I pour his drinks and then head over to see the kids.

"Hey Uncle Corbin."

Fran looks up from the coloring book she's working on. It's a robot coloring book, and she's using the metallic markers I got her for her birthday.

"Hey baby girl."

Fran's seven years old, but I still think of her as the baby. Fran was just one year old when her daddy passed away. She didn't know Paul, but I've done my best to keep his memory alive for her.

Her brother was four, and the loss hit him harder.

"How did the science project go?" I ask Jamie.

He keeps his eyes on the book he's reading.

"Good."

Jamie worked on his science project all weekend, and I helped him glue the planets together. He took it into school this morning nervous for the presentation.

"Just good? Did you present today?"

"Yeah."

"What did the teacher say?"

"She said it was good."

Jeez, it's like pulling teeth getting this one to talk.

"What did she like about it?"

He puts his book down and turns his attention to me.

"She liked that I included all the dwarf planets and not just the big ones." His face lights up for the first time since he got back from school. "She said my research was thorough, especially about the moons in Jupiter and which ones we might find life on."

A smile creeps across my face.

"That's awesome, dude. I know you put so much work into it."

It was a shock to me when Jamie turned out to love books and science. His father was the most charismatic man I've ever met. Paul could talk to anyone and light up any room. Paul loved sports. He was the school quarterback and played baseball in the summer. Paul was all action and high energy, but his son didn't inherit those genes.

Jamie is as quiet as Paul was loud. He's often got his head buried in a book, and science is his favorite subject at school.

I used to take him out to kick a ball around, but I

finally had to concede that he's not interested in sports. I tried to think about what Paul would want for his son. Would he want him to follow in his footsteps, be athletic and have a military career? But I concluded he'd want Jamie to follow his own passions, whatever those might be.

So I've helped Angie encourage him in those areas. I helped him with the science project he put together in the restaurant while Angie worked.

Jamie may look like the spitting image of his father, but that's where the similarities end. He's a different kid, but I hope one his father would be proud of.

I spend the next hour helping the kids with their homework while Angie takes over the bar.

She preps for the evening shift, and I stay until five when the night staff arrives.

"All right, kids, time to go."

She looks weary, and I ache to take her in my arms and smooth her worries away. But as usual I push my feelings down, smiling at the kids as they pack up their things.

"What's for dinner, Mom?" Fran asks.

"I don't know, honey. Something simple tonight."

"Not beans on toast again." Fran scrunches up her nose.

"Do we have any lasagna left over?" Jamie asks hopefully.

Once a week I make something for Angie and bring it around. She's too busy to make the kids homemade meals. I wasn't a cook before I left the military, but in those first few grief stricken years, Angie wasn't eating properly and so I stepped in.

"I'm making shepherd's pie this week; I'll drop one off tomorrow."

Angie gives me a grateful look. "You don't have to keep doing that, you know."

"I know. But if I don't make sure you all eat properly, Paul will kill me when I get to heaven."

She smiles, and her smile can still make butterflies flutter in my chest.

"Why don't you join us for dinner tonight. I've got nuggets and fries in the freezer. It's not much, but...." She shrugs her shoulders. "It would be nice to feed you after all you've done for us today."

I shake my head. Even though I want nothing more than to go upstairs to Angie's apartment above the bar and sit across from her at the dinner table, to watch her eat and listen to the kids chatter, it would be crossing a line.

I promised Paul I'd look after Angie and the kids. I help at the bar, I help with homework, I try to be a strong male influence in their lives. But breaking bread at the dinner table is a step too far. I'm afraid I wouldn't want to leave. That it would be too cozy and intimate and feel too much like a family. I'm afraid that I'd give in to my desires and tell Angie how I feel.

I promised Paul I'd look after his wife; it would be a disgrace to his memory to make a move on her.

So as always, I shrug off dinner while promising to bring something homemade for them to eat tomorrow.

Angie gives me a kiss on the cheek, and for one glorious moment I catch a whiff of her peppermint bodywash and feminine aroma.

I breathe deep, savoring her scent and the brush of her lips on my cheek. It was a chaste kiss, but I'll cling to the memory of it when I'm alone in bed tonight.

With a smile plastered on my face, I watch as the three people I love more than anything in the world head home without me.

To keep reading visit:
mybook.to/CherishedbytheMountain

GET YOUR FREE BOOKS

Sign up to the Sadie King mailing list and get access to all the bonus content including bonus scenes and five FREE steamy short romances!

You'll be the first to hear about new releases, exclusive offers, bonus content and all my news. You can even email me back. I love chatting with my readers!

To claim your free ebooks visit:
authorsadieking.com/bonus-scenes

If you're already a subscriber check your last email for the link that will take you straight to the bonus content.

ABOUT THE AUTHOR

Sadie King is a USA Today Best Selling Author of over 120 short and steamy contemporary romances. She loves writing about military heroes and the sassy women who heal their hearts.

Sadie lives in New Zealand with her ex-military husband and raucous young son.

When she's not writing she loves catching waves with her son, running along the beach, and drinking good wine, preferably with a book in hand.

Sign up to her newsletter to receive all the latest news and releases and access to exclusive bonus content.

www.authorsadieking.com